Forest Fairies

Nova Shimmers

MADDY MARA
Author of Dragon Girls

By Maddy Mara

Forever Fairies

DRAGON GIRLS

DRAGON GAMES

Forever Fairies

Nova Shimmers

by Maddy Mara

SCHOLASTIC

Published in the UK by Scholastic, 2024
1 London Bridge, London, SE1 9BG
Scholastic Ireland, 89E Lagan Road, Dublin Industrial Estate, Glasnevin, Dublin, D11 HP5F

SCHOLASTIC and associated logos are trademarks and/or
registered trademarks of Scholastic Inc.

First published in the US by Scholastic Inc., 2024

ISBN 978 0702 33739 0

A CIP catalogue record for this book is available from the British Library.

Printed and bound in Great Britain in Clays Ltd, Elcograf S.p.A.
Paper made from wood grown in sustainable forests and other controlled sources.

1 3 5 7 9 10 8 6 4 2

www.scholastic.co.uk

All the fairies were fast asleep. All the fairies, that is, but one. Nova the Sprout Wing had just woken up. She was confused. *Where am I?*

Nova sat up and looked around. *Oh, that's right. The bedroom branch in the Forever Tree!*

Until recently, Nova had been curled inside her

flower, growing and growing. Her tulip had sung her songs and whispered stories, helping Nova learn the ways of the Magic Forest. Two days ago, on the first day of spring, Nova had sprouted! And so had three other fairies: Lulu, Coco and Zali. The four new fairies were called Sprout Wings – and now they lived in the Forever Tree with all the other, bigger Forever Fairies.

The fairies hadn't known one another for long, but it already felt like they'd be friends for life. *It's because we sprouted on the same day,* decided Nova. *That makes us forever friends.*

Morning was just breaking, but Nova knew it would be a while before anyone else awoke. Even the glow bee on night-light duty had his eyes shut.

She tried reading the book she'd borrowed from the library branch. But she couldn't focus – her brain was whirring! She kept thinking about the fairy pods. There were the Flutterflies, the Shimmerbuds, the Twinklestars and the Sparkleberries. Which pod would she be put in? And what about her friends? Nova knew it all depended on how they each did in the pod trials.

Yesterday, Nova and the other Sprout Wings had finished their very first trial. It was for the Flutterfly pod. They had all done well, but Lulu was definitely the best flyer. Next up was Shimmerbud! This was the pod that looked after the creatures of the Magic Forest.

Nova couldn't stay in bed a moment longer. She decided she would watch the sunrise while she waited for everyone else to wake up. Very quietly, she tiptoed across the smooth wooden floor and opened a window. The delicious smells of the Magic Forest filled her little nose. Nova stretched her wings and flew out of the window into the cool air.

All around, the forest was slowly coming to life. There were the low buzz of insects and the happy chirping of birds. Nova listened to their intricate songs. One bird in particular caught her attention. Its whistle was so happy that it made her want to dance! Nova pursed her lips and tried to copy the sound.

Not quite right... She tried again, and this time she was much closer!

Just then she heard someone else whistle. Looking about, Nova saw a creature sitting on a nearby branch. A troll! She had green hair tied into high bunches and dark-green freckles splashed across her green face. In fact, the only part of her that wasn't green was the very tip of her nose, which was pink.

The troll waved at Nova. "Early riser, huh? I'm the same. How can anyone lie in bed when there's a whole forest waiting to be explored? You're good at bird sounds. That's a gleebird you just imitated. I've been trying for ages to copy it. I'm Lex, by the way."

"I'm Nova," said Nova, fluttering over. "Mind if I join you?"

Nova wasn't normally chatty, but she was very excited to meet a troll. When she was growing in her flower, Nova had loved hearing stories about

trolls. She knew they were a lot more mischievous than fairies, but they loved the Magic Forest just the same. Nova and the other Sprout Wings had already met a pair of trolls called Tex and Rox. But this troll was new and exciting and ...

"Achoo!"

... unwell?

"Wow! That was my biggest sneeze yet." Lex pulled out a giant green hanky and blew her nose loudly. "As you can see, I have a cold. But don't worry – I won't sneeze on you. You're one of the Sprout Wings, right? Do you know which pod you're going to be in?"

"Not yet," said Nova. "We're still doing trials."

Lex swung her legs back and forth. "If I were a fairy, I'd want to be in the pod that looks after the forest's creatures. You know, the one that makes remedies and medicines for the sick and injured animals?"

"That's the Shimmerbud pod," Nova said. "They wear the purple-and-green costumes. We're doing their trial next."

Nova was still learning about the different pods, but she had to agree with Lex: the Shimmerbuds sounded wonderful.

"That's the one." Lex nodded. "They run the hospital burrow under the Forever Tree. We often take wounded creatures there if we can tell they need fairy medicine more than troll medicine."

"Trolls make medicine, too?" Nova asked.

"Of course!" Lex sounded proud. "It's not the same as fairy medicine because trolls don't do magic like fairies do. But we use ancient troll knowledge, and our remedies are very powerful. I am on my way to pick tangfruits now, actually. Tangfruit juice is an important ingredient in our cold remedy."

Nova was about to ask Lex what else was in the troll remedy when she heard a tinkling bell.

Lex laughed. "There's always a bell ringing somewhere in the fairy world! What does that one mean?"

"I think it's the breakfast bell. I'd better get going." Nova was reluctant to leave – she wanted to stay and chat with Lex. But Nova was not a very fast flyer, and she didn't like being late.

She spread her wings wide and rose into the air. "It was very nice meeting you, Lex!"

The troll let out another explosive sneeze. This one was so loud it shook the leaves. Lex grinned at Nova. "Nice to meet you, too. I'd better go and pick that tangfruit before my next sneeze knocks over the Forever Tree!"

The other fairies were just waking up when Nova

flew back through the window.

"There you are!" called Zali, the smallest of the

four fairies. She was still in bed, yawning. "Where

were you?"

"I went to watch the sunrise," Nova explained.

"And I met a troll called Lex. She told me about troll medicine."

"You should have woken us!" cried Lulu, bouncing out of bed. "I love meeting trolls!"

Lulu was always full of energy. Not only could she fly twice as fast as her friends, but she did somersaults and spins as she flew, just for the fun of it.

"Should we go on a little adventure now?" Coco suggested, her eyes bright. She was always enthusiastic and quick with an idea.

"No time for sky-larking!" buzzed the glow bee from above. "It's breakfast time. And someone is coming."

There was a friendly knock on the door. Lulu

cartwheeled across the room to open it. A fairy dressed in a purple top and leaf-green skirt stepped in. It was Vida, the Alpha Wing – or head fairy – of the Shimmerbud pod. Flowers were threaded through Vida's wavy chestnut hair, and a shiny *A* was embroidered on her top.

"Morning, Sprouties," Vida said in her calm way. On her arm was a basket covered with a purple cloth. There was a delicious smell of blossoms and nectar.

"Ooh, breakfast!" Zali said, jumping out of bed. "I'm starving!"

"Me too." Coco eyed the basket hungrily. "What are we having today?"

"Floatmeal." Vida set down the basket on the table. She whisked off the cloth to reveal a steaming bowl.

"Floatmeal is very popular in our branch," Vida explained. "But you'll need to eat quickly. It has a habit of trying to escape. Look, there it goes now."

The creamy, sparkly mixture was slowly rising into the air. Expertly, Vida pushed the floatmeal back down with a wooden ladle and dished it into four smaller bowls.

"Come and eat while it's hot," Vida said. "And before it sticks to the ceiling!"

"So, what are we doing today?" Zali asked Vida as they ate.

"You'll be busy," Vida said. "First, we must collect your Shimmerbud costumes. Then there's a tour of the tree. You also have an important training session for the Shimmerbud trial tomorrow."

Coco posed the question they were all dying to ask. "What do we have to do for the trial?"

"I can't reveal much." Vida's eyes twinkled mysteriously. "But I can say you four will need to work together, gathering ingredients to make a special Shimmerbud remedy."

Nova loved the sound of finding ingredients to make a remedy with her friends!

"You will need to work quickly," Vida continued. "Shimmerbuds often have to do things at great speed, with many things happening all at once. So we always have a time limit for our trial."

Oh dear! This was not great news for Nova. She had only sprouted a few days ago, but it was already clear that speed was not something she was naturally good at.

"But first up, let's head to the costume branch," Vida said. "Have you all finished?"

"I have," Coco said.

"I finished ages ago," Lulu said. "It was delicious!"

"Um, Nova?" Zali giggled. "Your floatmeal is heading for the window."

Nova had been so busy thinking about the Shimmerbud trial that she'd forgotten to keep an eye on her floatmeal. She jumped up and chased her breakfast, catching it with her spoon and managing to eat it before it escaped.

"Now I'm finished!" she said.

Vida pulled out her silver wand and made the breakfast mess vanish. The clean bowls returned themselves to the basket, and all the stray lumps of floatmeal disappeared.

The Sprout Wings had been given wands, but they didn't know how to use them yet. Nova already liked holding hers – it thrummed with power and magic. She planned to keep her wand tucked into whatever she was wearing, like the bigger fairies did.

"OK, Sprouties," Vida said, heading for the door. "We're off. But first, remind me: what's the rule about the stairs?"

"No flying!" chorused the Sprout Wings as they followed Vida out of their branch.

The curving inner walls of the tree were lined with more stairs than were possible to count. At least, Nova hadn't managed it yet. But one day she would, she was sure of it!

"What does the floor look like today?" Coco wondered out loud.

The fairies peered down at the glittering floor far below. It was made up of hundreds of gleaming gemstones. The pattern changed constantly, depending on what was happening in the tree. Today it was all green swirls and glorious purple flowers.

"Shimmerbud colours," Zali observed.

Vida nodded. "And the colour of the costumes

we're about to collect. We're almost there now!"

Vida led the little group up the staircase. As the fairies climbed, the steps sounded musical notes, each one higher than the last. It made going up and down the tree's stairs much more fun!

Lulu, who never ran out of steam, was up front. Coco was behind her, chatting away and asking Vida questions. Even Zali, who was humming and looking around as she climbed, was faster than Nova.

Nova sighed. *Why am I always so slow?*

Finally, Vida stopped climbing and knocked at a purple door.

"Come in!" called a cheerful voice.

The costume branch was filled to the brim.

Stacked to one side were bolts of shining, colourful fabric. Chests overflowing with buttons and ribbons lined the walls. And everywhere Nova looked were spools of thread, twitching at the ends like they couldn't wait to be made into something wonderful.

"This is as good as the craft branch! Maybe even better." Zali's eyes shone. "Look up there!"

Hanging from the ceiling were all kinds of outfits in every imaginable style, size and shape. The whole branch looked like an upside-down garden of beautiful blooms made from all kinds of fabrics.

There was so much to take in that Nova jumped when she heard a voice call, "Hello, Sprout Wings!"

The fairy wore a patchwork smock and had several large needles sticking out of her ponytail. A tape measure was draped round her neck.

"This is Mave," said Vida. "You met her when you first sprouted, remember? Mave is the Sparkleberry Alpha Wing."

Mave smiled. "It's great to see you all again. And guess what! I've just finished your Shimmerbud costumes. Try them on!"

Mave gave each of the Sprouties a shimmering pile

of purple and green clothes.

Nova pulled on her costume: a purple dress

shaped like a blossom and a leaf-green sleeveless

jacket. The dress was a little bit too big, but it

quickly shrank to fit her. Nova turned this way

and that, admiring her new outfit. It felt so right!

"And here are your hats. Catch!" Mave spun four leafy hats into the air.

The Sprout Wings leapt up to grab them.

"You'd be surprised how often they come in handy," Vida said.

"Are there different sizes?" Zali's voice was muffled—because her tiny face was completely covered by her giant hat! Everyone burst out laughing. Zali rose into the air and began to fly around, arms outstretched theatrically.

"Why is it so dark?" she joked. "Have the glow bees gone home? Where are you all?"

Coco darted into the air. "I'm over here! Catch

me if you can!"

Zali spun round and headed in the direction of Coco's voice, the huge hat still covering her eyes.

Coco squealed and flew in the opposite direction.

"Try and get me!" called Lulu, joining in the game.

So Zali started chasing after Lulu instead. But Lulu was much too fast, easily zipping out of her way.

"Nova, are you playing?" Zali asked.

Nova glanced over at the Alpha Wings. Were they annoyed by the game? But Vida and Mave were laughing, so Nova flew into the air. "Over here!"

In a flash, Zali turned and flew in her direction. But Nova was in a corner and had no chance of getting away. Just before Zali reached out to grab her, Nova made a special buzzing sound.

Zali stopped mid-air. "Oops! Sorry!"

Everyone laughed, and Zali pulled off her hat. She stared at Nova. "You sounded exactly like a glow bee! How did you do that?"

"I don't know," Nova admitted.

"Can you do any other sounds?" Lulu asked. "Like birds?"

Nova remembered the birdsong she'd heard that morning. She thought for a moment, then began to whistle.

"Wow! A perfect gleebird!" Mave clapped.

There was a sudden pulsing light from Vida's wand.

Coco leaned over. "The flower symbol on your wand is flashing!"

"The Shimmerbud symbol lighting up means a new patient has arrived in the hospital burrow," Vida explained. "I'd better go."

"Can we come?" Nova asked.

"Exactly what I was going to ask! Can we? Please?" Coco begged.

Vida considered this. "Well ... we do have your training down there soon. If you're interested, then why not?"

The Sprouties jumped up and down with excitement. They thanked Mave and dashed out of the costume branch after Vida.

"Squirrel pox has been going around," Vida said as they hurried down the stairs. The musical notes descended as they went. "And the song spiders often get sore throats this time of year. I just hope one of the skating bears hasn't twisted an ankle again."

"You can fit a whole bear in your hospital?" Nova was amazed. "I didn't realize the place was so big."

"Goodness no! We shrink the larger patients down to size," Vida explained. "It's important to reapply the shrinking spell every night. One evening we forgot to re-shrink a rainbow sheep. The next morning, it was like a giant, woolly rainbow had moved in!"

The more Vida told them about the hospital, the more Nova wanted to see it!

"It's underground, right?" Lulu asked. She was the only one who was comfortably keeping up with Vida. She wasn't even out of breath!

"Correct," Vida said as they reached ground level.

Vida moved to the centre of the huge space. "Gather round, but don't stand on that gold flower."

Nova, who was standing right where Vida pointed, hastily moved aside. Vida pulled out her wand and used it to draw the shape of a flower in the air.

The golden petals on the floor unfolded, revealing a perfect circle. Light streamed up from the hole, along with the sound of distant voices. The air smelled like nectar and rich soil and lush leaves all crushed together. It was a powerful smell, yet somehow soothing.

"What is this?" Coco was examining a pole in the middle of the circle.

"That's the slidey-pole," Vida explained. "Grab hold of it, tuck in your wings and slide!"

Lulu went first. "Whee!" she yelled as she disappeared. Coco went next, followed by Zali.

Nova's heart thumped as she grabbed the pole.

"Go on," urged Vida. "It's almost as fun as flying!"

Nova whooshed down, laughing with the pleasure of it. Vida was right – what a way to travel!

Nova landed next to her friends. What had been the floor now glittered above them like a stained-glass ceiling.

"Welcome to the hospital burrow," said Vida,

landing neatly beside them.

Nova looked around. The large, brightly lit room was full of activity and life. Shimmerbud fairies flittered from bed to bed, tending to the patients. In one area, Nova saw squirrels with oddly spotted tails. In another were butterflies and dragonflies, many with bandaged wings or antennae. There were a couple of fairy patients, too, propped up on soft pillows.

I want to know about them all! thought Nova. *Does that squirrel's tail hurt? How do you bandage a wing?* It looked complicated.

A familiar troll hurried over, something fluffy in her green arms.

"Hi, Lex," said Nova. "You look better already!" Lex's nose was no longer pink.

"My troll remedy fixed me up real quick," said Lex.

"You know each other?" Vida asked.

"We had a sunrise chat." Lex winked at Nova. "Vida, I found this bunny when I was foraging. She has a snarlthorn in her paw. I tried to get it out, but I think it calls for fairy magic."

Vida gave the bunny a soothing pat and pulled out her wand. "Don't worry, we'll get that out in no time."

The snarlthorn growled and squirmed, trying to duck away. But Vida expertly tapped her wand directly on the burr. With a little crackle, the thorn disappeared.

Wow! thought Nova. *Fairy medicine is truly amazing*

Vida barely had time to tuck away her wand before a Flutterfly fairy swooshed over. She was holding a basket that seemed to be sneezing and coughing.

"A bout of snufflebug sniffles!" the fairy announced, setting down the basket.

The Sprout Wings leaned in closer. Two miserable-looking bugs with red noses and watery eyes gazed up at them.

One sneezed dramatically. "I might be dying."

"I'll never feel well again," moaned the other.

A smile twitched at Vida's mouth. "Any fever or headaches?"

"No. But I feel terrible!" wailed the first bug.

"I feel terribler," said the second.

"Have you been playing in the cold without your scarves?" Vida asked.

The snufflebugs looked guilty.

"That's how bugs get bugs," Vida tutted.

"Trolls have a great cold remedy," said Lex. "Shall I make a batch?"

Vida shook her head. "Thanks, but we have our

fairy remedy."

Lex shrugged. "If you change your mind, let me know. It's not magical like a fairy cure, but it's very powerful." She waved goodbye.

Nova gazed after Lex. She got the feeling the troll was disappointed. Nova was, too. She wanted to learn all about fairy medicine, but she was also curious about troll remedies!

"Treatment time!" announced a fairy wheeling in a cart laden with bottles of all different shapes and sizes.

"Excuse me!" called a butterfly from nearby. "My wing bandage is slipping off."

"Could I have some more nectar?" asked a

dragonfly. "I'm so thirsty!"

The snufflebugs sneezed loudly again.

There was A LOT going on!

"Sprouties," said Vida, "it's time to start your training. But, as you can see, the hospital is rather busy this morning."

"We could help out." Nova looked at Lulu, Coco and Zali. "Couldn't we?"

The others nodded enthusiastically.

"We can do our training after things calm down," Coco added.

Vida smiled. "Thank you. After all, there's nothing like learning on the job!"

The Sprouties headed for the potions cart.

"Three drops of acorn remedy for the squirrels," instructed a fairy, pointing to a tiny blue bottle of sparkling liquid.

"Midsummer pine nectar for the butterflies, dragonflies and hummingbirds," another fairy explained. "Two drops per patient. And this is a carrot elixir for that little bunny. She can have as much as she wants."

Nova had just finished giving a hummingbird some pine nectar when Vida called her over. She was looking after a tiny white mouse whose tail was bent at a funny angle.

"It hurts!" The mouse's whiskers trembled.

"Nova, can you hold him steady while I do a

wrapping spell?"

Nova smiled at the mouse as she gently held his tail. "Don't worry. Vida is an expert."

Vida tapped a tightly rolled bandage with her wand. It promptly unwrapped itself, the end rising into the air. Vida made a circular motion with her wand, and the bandage wrapped neatly round the mouse's tail.

"That feels better already!" squeaked the mouse.

"Pleased to hear it," said Vida, tucking the mouse into a cosy bed. Then she called, "Sprouties, now let's get to the Shimmerlab for your training!"

Lulu, Zali and Coco finished what they were doing and fluttered over.

Nova felt a strange mix of emotions. On the one wing, she was excited about the training. But on the other, she didn't want to leave the hospital. It felt good to be helping.

"I am going to teach you some spells so you're ready for the trial tomorrow," Vida explained.

"We're learning spells?" Zali looked thrilled.

"Like actual, genuine spells?" Lulu asked.

"Using our wands?" Coco added.

Vida laughed. "Yes, yes and yes!"

They left the hustle and bustle of the hospital and travelled down a narrow tunnel barely big enough to fly through.

Vida came to a stop in front of a round wooden

door. She swished her wand, and it magically swung open.

Nova and the other Sprout Wings gazed around the room. The Shimmerlab was almost as big as the hospital burrow. Shelves lined the curved walls from floor to ceiling. They were crammed with all kinds of interesting things: dried berries and flowers, colourful bark, glass jars filled with sparkling powders and bubbling liquids. There were big scoops and tiny spoons, as well as jugs, scales, pincers and pots. Curious, magical smells hung in the air.

In the centre was a large wooden table, worn and ancient-looking. It was piled with rolled bandages and trays of leaves, berries, bark and stones.

Vida fluttered to the head of the table. "First, I'll teach you the bandage-winding spell," she announced. "We are going to practise on one of our own wings. Be careful! It's easy to get tangled. Watch closely."

Vida performed the same steps she'd done earlier on the mouse, wrapping a bandage neatly round her left wing.

"The secret is to think very clearly about where you want the bandage to go," Vida explained. "And you must tap it with your wand in just the right way: not too hard, not too soft. Then your wand swirls have to be even and very round. Give it a try!"

Eagerly, the four fairies pulled out their wands. Nova felt hers quiver, as if it were just as excited as she was to be learning magic!

Nova tapped it on a rolled-up bandage. To her delight, the gauzy fabric rose into the air. It was working! Next, Nova drew a careful circle. But the bandage did not wrap round her wing – it wrapped round her wrist. Nova untied the bandage and tried again. This time, it wrapped round her ankle.

Nova sighed. The spell was harder than it looked! *I need to think more clearly about what I want to bandage.*

She untied the material from her ankle. Closing

her eyes, she pictured the bandage wrapping round her wing. She imagined every little fold and turn. She even imagined it tucking in its final loose end.

When Nova opened her eyes and tried the spell again, the bandage did exactly what she wanted.

"Wow! How did you do that?" Lulu cried. She

was entirely tangled up!

Lulu wasn't the only one finding it difficult. Coco and Zali also had their bandages wrapped in all the wrong places.

"You're a natural!" Coco said, unwinding a loop from her neck.

Nova shook her head. "It took me plenty of tries to get it right." Still, it felt good not to be trailing behind the others for once.

With a little more practice, everyone perfected bandage winding.

"Next, we'll learn the move and mix," Vida announced, pulling a tray of ingredients and a golden bowl towards her. She firmly tapped each item with her wand: a pale crystal, a sprig of sweet-smelling blossom and a sliver of copper-coloured bark. With a flick of her wand, everything vanished – and reappeared in the golden bowl.

"That's the *move* part of the spell," Vida said. "And now for the fun part – *mix*!"

Vida tapped the side of the bowl with her wand and the metal hummed. She made a stirring motion in the air above the bowl. Slowly, the ingredients began to crumble and mix. Soon everything had dissolved into a fine powder.

"Now you try. And, with this spell, I'm giving you a time limit."

Nova hated feeling rushed. But then she thought about the creatures in the hospital burrow – the miserable snufflebugs, the injured bunny, that little mouse. *I'll just have to learn this, and quickly.*

The move-and-mix spell wasn't easy. And when their time was up, Nova had no idea if she had done the spell correctly.

Vida fluttered around the room inspecting everyone's mixtures.

"Yours needs a little more blossom, Zali. And, Lulu, yours has bits of rock in it. Try tapping a little more firmly next time." Vida nodded in approval at Coco. "Very good, Coco. Just make sure you don't rush the mixing part; it's a little clumpy."

Nova's heart thumped as Vida inspected the contents of her bowl. "Nova, yours is perfect. Well done!"

Vida taught the Sprout Wings a few more spells. One was for soothing strained wings – good for fairies, as well as all other winged creatures – and another was for making head bumps go down.

Then Vida took them on a tour of some of the Shimmerbuds' favourite places in the Forever Tree. Nova particularly loved the greenhouse branch, where the fairies grew herbs, fruit trees and other plants. Growing near the entrance was a lush-looking vine with dangling seeds of every colour imaginable.

Vida split open a pink one. "This is a glitter-plant," she explained as glitter spilled out. "We harvest the seeds and then dry them. We use glitter in countless ways – in cooking, medicine and for crafts. Glitterplants grow abundantly in the greenhouse. We grow far more than we can use – and that's saying something, given how much glitter Forever Fairies use."

"What's that scent?" Nova asked, flitting between the fruit trees. She could smell something lemony and peppery.

"That's the tangfruit." Vida showed Nova the few tiny, star-shaped fruits growing nearby.

"Tangfruit! Lex told me it's good for colds." Nova thought about how quickly the troll's cold had been cured.

Vida nodded. "But tangfruit is difficult to grow. We only get one small crop each year, so it's precious."

Next to the greenhouse was the Shimmerbud branch. This branch was far less tidy than the Flutterfly branch, which the Sprout Wings had visited a few days ago. The walls were lined with bookshelves, and there were more books in wonky piles all over the place. Lush plants grew in

hovering pots, and Shimmerbud fairies lounged on comfy couches, reading and sipping tea. There was an open fire, flickering magically with purple-blue flames. The whole pod felt calm and cosy.

By the time the Sprout Wings returned to their branch that evening, Nova was brimming with ideas and inspiration. But the other Sprouties looked exhausted! They had just enough energy to eat a supper of cheese, soup and bread that was waiting for them before falling into their cloud-soft beds.

"My head might explode with all the things we learned today." Zali sighed as she snuggled under her covers.

"Same," Lulu said. "I hope we can remember it

all tomorrow."

"We will," Coco said confidently. "And we can help one another out. Are you all looking forward to it?"

"For sure," Lulu replied sleepily.

"I am," said Nova. "But I'm a bit worried about the time limit. What about you, Zali?"

There was no reply from Zali. The smallest fairy was already fast asleep, snoring loudly.

🌷 🌷 🌷

Nova awoke as the sun was rising. Her dreams had been full of spells, the trial, and, mostly, the patients in the hospital burrow. *Are the snuffle-bugs better? Has the bunny's paw healed? How's the injured mouse?*

Although it was still quite dark, Nova got out of bed and slipped on her Shimmerbud dress and jacket. Grabbing her wand, she tiptoed past the glow bee dozing near the ceiling and quietly opened the door.

She didn't see any other fairies as she made her way downstairs. Even the musical stairs seemed quieter than usual.

On the ground level, she hurried over to the golden flower, carefully copying the door-opening gesture she'd seen Vida do with her wand. With a creak, the flower revealed the slidey-pole entrance down to the hospital burrow.

Nova tucked in her wings, grabbed the pole and

slid down. She expected the hospital to be as quiet as the rest of the tree. But far from it! As she landed, Nova heard laughter and was surprised to see Tex and Rox, the trolls who had played a trick during the Flutterfly trial.

What are they doing here? Nova wondered. She found trolls so intriguing.

Strangely, the trolls were doing cartwheels and backflips. At least, they were trying to. They kept tripping over each other and falling into tangled heaps, groaning dramatically.

Waves of laughter echoed throughout the burrow. The patients were sitting up in their beds, watching the trolls and grinning. Even the snufflebugs were smiling, although Nova got the feeling they were trying not to. Shimmerbud fairies bustled about, chuckling as they worked.

"The trolls often put on early morning shows for the patients," a passing fairy explained to Nova.

Now Tex and Rox were juggling some star-shaped things. Nova knew exactly what they were: precious tangfruit!

6

Just then, Vida appeared. She looked distracted.
"Our entire tangfruit supply has vanished," she
said.

Nova pointed at the juggling trolls. The floor
was covered in squished tangfruit, and the trolls
were dripping with juice.

Vida gasped as Tex flung the last remaining

tangfruit up high.

"I'll rescue it!" Nova zoomed into the air, reaching out her hands. But she wasn't fast enough, and the fruit plopped on to Tex's head. It split apart, and juice trickled down the troll's face.

With a wide grin, Tex stuck out his long green tongue and slurped it up.

"Mmm! Now I taste as good as I look!" he declared.

The patients erupted into gales of laughter.

Vida groaned, her face in her hands. "We needed those tangfruits! And now you've wasted them all."

A hush fell across the burrow.

The trolls folded their arms and glared at Vida.

"Typical fairies," grumbled Tex. "Worried about a bit of mess and a few squished fruits. Can't you see how much good our performance is doing? And not a word of gratitude!"

Vida folded her arms, too. "Of course we are grateful. But tangfruit is an important ingredient, and you have just wasted a year's supply!"

Tex and Rox wiped the juice from their faces.

"Well, there's no need for you to worry about us *wasting* any of your precious ingredients any more," Rox snapped. "Because we'll never perform in the hospital burrow again!"

With that, the two green creatures turned and stomped out.

Vida looked at Nova. "I forget how touchy the trolls can be sometimes. I know Tex and Rox mean well. But it's annoying they used up our tangfruit supply. On today of all days!"

Before Nova could ask Vida what she meant by that last comment, her friends came down the slidey-pole, one after the other.

Lulu landed lightly on her feet, followed by Coco and Zali. "We had a hunch we'd find you here!"

The patients waved happily at the Sprout Wings. They had clearly made a good impression the day before! The uncomfortable mood caused by the trolls storming off drifted away.

"We brought you breakfast," Zali said, holding out a slightly squished puff cake.

"Thanks!" Nova took a grateful bite, only now realizing how hungry she was.

Her friends were all dressed in their shiny Shimmerbud costumes. Nova was pleased to see that Zali's hat had finally shrunk to fit.

"Also, I've made these for the patients." Zali held out a selection of tiny homemade gifts. Nova, Lulu and Coco gathered round to see what their friend had created: a carrot with a smiley face for the bunny, a filmy shawl for the butterfly, a cheese-shaped pillow for the mouse. Zali had even made tiny scarves for the snufflebugs.

"Zali! These are wonderful!" Vida said, coming to look.

Nova was relieved to see that the Alpha was smiling again.

"You're so clever," said Coco. "I don't know when you found the time."

"I woke up in the middle of the night," said Zali, looking a little embarrassed by the praise. "It was fun."

Nova gave the little fairy a hug. Her friends were the best!

After Zali and the others had handed out the presents, Vida reminded them that the Shimmerbud trial was about to start.

"Just let me get changed." Vida pointed her wand at her head and swished it back and forth, all the way down to her toes. There was a twinkle of stars, and suddenly Vida was dressed in her formal flounce wear.

The Sprouties said goodbye to everyone in the

hospital burrow.

"Good luck!" called one of the Shimmerbuds. "Thanks for all your help!"

Even the patients seemed excited about the trial. "We'll be cheering for you!" they called, clutching their gifts to their chests.

"Sorry, but we won't be cheering." The snufflebugs sniffed. "Our throats are *really* sore today."

Vida tapped on a door with her wand, and it promptly swung open. "This is a shortcut to the surface. There are loads of tunnels all through the Magic Forest – most are made by trolls. They're experts in tunnelling."

Excitement and nerves whirled inside Nova

as the Sprouties flew through the tunnel behind Vida. She really wanted to do well in this trial.

As the fairies popped out near the base of the tree, they were greeted by hundreds of cheering fairies. Some were flying and some were sitting on the broad branches above, their legs swinging as they chatted and laughed. There was a festive feel in the air. Even the Forever Tree was dressed in its finest purple flowers and bright green leaves!

"I'll be right back. You can warm up your wands while you wait." Vida disappeared into the crowd.

The little fairies pulled out their wands. "Let's tap

them together and see what happens," said Lulu.

The four fairies gently tapped wands. Instantly, a magical puff of smoke bloomed into the air and settled over them.

Nova felt a calm confidence spread through her. It was as though their wands were sending them good luck.

"I feel less nervous," Zali said.

"Same," Coco said.

"Maybe it's because we bonded them after the Flutterfly trial?" Nova suggested. "Maybe we got extra wand power!"

"I'm going to need extra power if we have to remember all the spells Vida taught us yesterday."

Lulu recklessly waved her wand around.

"Careful!" Coco laughed. "You nearly clonked me. I don't want you doing a move-and-mix spell with my hair!"

7

Vida reappeared through the crowd. "The Forever Wings are ready for you!"

The group flew over the crowd of fairies until they reached four graceful, older fairies sitting at a floating platform. These were the Forever Wings, the leaders of the four pods. They were also the judges of the trials.

Each elder was dressed in the colours of her pod: pink and aqua for Sparkleberry, silver and gold for Twinklestar, and the Flutterfly elder wore yellow and blue. The Shimmerbud elder was dressed in green and purple like the Sprout Wings – and the Forever Tree! Her silvery hair was tied in an elegant bun.

The Forever Wings smiled warmly at the Sprouties. The elders were very grand and important, but they were much less scary when they smiled like that.

"Welcome to your second trial," said the Shimmerbud elder. "I trust you have learned the

spells you need?"

"We have," Coco said. "But we don't know what we have to do with them yet."

"We can reveal that now," replied the elder. "You four must make a sore throat remedy."

"A *real* remedy? For a *real* patient?" Zali squeaked.

"What if we get it wrong?" Lulu asked nervously.

Nova felt the same. This was their first-ever remedy, after all. She didn't want to make some poor patient feel worse!

The Shimmerbud elder smiled kindly. "We will test your remedy before it goes anywhere near the patients. Speaking of patients, I can hear yours coming."

Nova could hear something, too. It sounded like coughing and complaining! As the crowd parted, a Shimmerbud appeared holding the snufflebugs' basket.

The Shimmerbud elder leaned forward. "How are you feeling, snufflebugs?"

"Worse than ever!" moaned one, giving a loud cough.

"My throat is on fire," whispered another.

"Never fear," said the elder. "These young fairies are going to make you a sore throat remedy." To the Sprouties she said, "You must complete your remedy by the time the sun is directly overhead. Vida, do you have the list of ingredients?"

Vida fluttered forward, holding a scroll of paper. Nova thought the Alpha looked worried.

Vida cleared her throat and read, "'For the Forever Fairy Sore Throat Remedy, you will need grated fireroot...'"

"We can get that from the kitchen branch,"

Coco whispered.

"'Morning leaf, crushed...'"

"That's easy," murmured Lulu.

"'A big pinch of golden glitter...'"

Zali beamed. "I know where to get that!"

Nova started to relax. Maybe this wouldn't be so hard after all.

Vida stopped reading and looked at the elders. "There's a problem with the last ingredient. It's tangfruit juice."

The Shimmerbud elder looked puzzled. "Last time I looked, we had a number of them growing in the greenhouse branch."

"We've had a hiccup with our supply," Vida said.

"The trolls used them all. For, um, juggling."

"Let me guess." The elder sighed. "They were putting on a show for the patients?"

Vida nodded. "To be fair, it cheered everyone up. But now we're out of tangfruit!"

The Shimmerbud elder tapped her chin thoughtfully. "Sprout Wings, would you like to make a different remedy for the trial?"

Nova looked at the miserable snufflebugs. "I think we should at least try to make the remedy that these patients need."

The elder gave her a pleased look. "Excellent Shimmerbud instincts. Do you have any ideas or solutions to suggest?"

Nova stared in surprise. Why was this wise elder asking them? They were just fresh little Sprouties!

But Nova realized she actually *did* have an idea. "I think there are tangfruit growing in the wild. Lex, one of the trolls, told me she was going to pick some for a troll remedy. She must have found some – she was healthy again the next time I saw her!"

The elders spoke among themselves in quiet tones for a few moments.

The Shimmerbud elder turned back. "Tangfruit has never thrived in the greenhouse. So, yes, let's take inspiration from this troll. Please pick a wild tangfruit – that is, if you're up to the challenge of finding one?"

"For sure we are!" replied Coco, bouncing on her toes.

"Nova will sniff one out," said Zali.

"Exactly!" added Lulu. "Nova has the best nose around. And not just because it's cute!"

The Forever Wings chuckled.

"We can try," Nova said. She was not sure she'd be able to sniff out a tangfruit. But her friends seemed confident!

"I didn't know tangfruit grew in the wild," said Vida.

"Oh, no young fairies do," the Shimmerbud elder said. "We've used greenhouse ones for such a long time. But finding a wild one adds a nice extra challenge to today's trial. I am confident these little fairies are up to it!"

"So am I." Vida smiled proudly at the Sprouties.

"What's taking so long?" moaned a snufflebug. "We're in SO much pain!"

Vida handed Nova a bag for collecting ingredients. Peeking inside, Nova saw collecting tubes, little pouches for soft herbs and lots of pockets.

"Good luck, Sprout Wings," said the Shimmerbud elder. "This is not an easy task. But you have one another, and that makes all the difference."

"Go, Sprouties!" cheered all the fairies as Nova, Coco, Lulu and Zali fluttered into the air.

"Goodbye," croaked the snufflebugs. "We may

have lost our voices completely by the time you return. But we are happy to use our last few words on you."

8

"Let's start with the morning leaf," suggested Lulu.

"I'll lead the way!"

The little Sprout Wings zoomed higher and higher, weaving through the branches of the enormous Forever Tree. Lulu, of course, was the fastest. And Nova, of course, was at the back.

When they reached the top branch, Lulu picked

the very highest leaf. "This is the first leaf to be touched by the sun each dawn. See? It's even tinged pink and gold."

"Great," said Nova, popping the leaf into a little pocket inside the bag. They had their first ingredient already!

Next, Coco led the way into the tree to the main kitchen branch. Normally, the fairy kitchens were bustling with activity. Twinklestars were always busy cooking delicious things for the whole tree. But today the main kitchen was almost deserted. All the fairies were outside, watching the trial.

Coco quickly found the stores of fireroot. "I love how it's shaped like a flame," she commented, handing the bright orange root to Nova.

"And it's warm!" noted Nova.

With two ingredients safely collected, the Sprout Wings headed to the craft branch. Zali promptly zipped behind a bolt of fabric and reappeared triumphantly with a bottle of gold glitter.

Nova held a collecting tube steady while Zali poured in the glitter, filling the tube right to the top.

"Is that too much?" wondered Nova.

"Nova," said Zali seriously. "You can never have too much glitter."

"Now we just need that wild tangfruit," said Coco.

"Yep, *just* something we have no idea how to find!" Nova sighed, feeling nervous all of a sudden.

"We'll find one," Lulu said confidently. "There are a lot of trees just beyond this grove. Shall we start there? Nova, you fly up next to me and let me know if you get any whiffs of tangfruit."

The Sprout Wings flew back out of the Forever Tree and over the crowd of watching fairies.

Everyone cheered and whooped as they passed. "You can do this, Sprouties!"

Nova hoped they were right! It was strange to be flying at the front of the group. But, to her surprise, she wasn't struggling to keep up with Lulu. Flying wing to wing with the fastest fairy seemed to help. *And being excited is giving me extra speed, too!*

On their Sprout Day, the four fairies had flown through the forest on their way to the Forever Tree. But that trip had been with Etta, the Flutterfly Alpha. This time felt different. Firstly, it was just the four of them. And secondly, they had an important mission to complete!

As they sped along, Nova tried to concentrate

on the smells of the forest. At first, there was no hint of tangfruit. But then, faintly, Nova began to pick up the now familiar lemony-peppery aroma. Gradually, the scent grew stronger until Nova was sure that tangfruits were nearby.

"Down there," she called, pointing to a cluster of trees in a valley below.

"OK, everyone. Get ready to land!" Lulu cried.

The fairies swooped lower, and Nova saw that one tree was MUCH bigger than the one struggling in the greenhouse. Its highest branches were dripping with enormous star-shaped fruit!

The fairies landed on the lush grass below the spectacular tree.

"Great work!" Coco said. "Let's pick a ripe tangfruit and get back. We've got a sore throat remedy to make!"

"Not so fast, little fairies," said a gruff voice.

A band of trolls stepped into view. Their green arms were crossed, and Nova spotted huffy-looking Tex and Rox in among the others.

"These are OUR trees. What makes you think you can steal OUR fruit?" demanded the biggest, meanest-looking troll.

Nova gulped. Zali and Lulu also looked nervous.

But Coco stood her ground. "You don't own these trees," she said firmly. "Everything in the Magic Forest belongs to everyone. Anyway, it's because

of you trolls that we've run out of tangfruit!"

From their grumpy faces, Nova could tell that the trolls did not like this one bit!

She thought fast. "Excuse me, but how do you get this tree to grow so well? It's wonderful! The tangfruit tree in our greenhouse isn't nearly so healthy. And its fruit is much smaller."

The big troll softened a little. "Tangfruit trees grow better outside. They're like trolls: they need to feel the earth beneath them and the sky above them."

Nova nodded. "That makes sense. I wonder, would it be possible for us to take just one fruit? We need it to make a remedy for two unwell snufflebugs."

The biggest troll looked furious all over again. "Why should we let you do that?" he roared. "Tex and Rox said you fairies were extremely rude this morning. And they were trying to help! For all we know, you'll just be rude again after we help you now."

Just then, a smaller troll pushed to the front. It was Lex. She was the only troll who didn't look angry. "Let them have one, Pa," she said, taking hold of the bigger troll's arm. "I don't think the fairies meant to be rude. And, besides, you like snufflebugs!"

The big troll paused. "It's true that snufflebugs are useful in our garden. And they're quite friendly when not sick." He looked at Tex and Rox. "What do you two think?"

Tex and Rox began whispering. Then they began giggling. Finally, Rox announced, "We are *terribly* offended, of course. But we say let the fairies pick a tangfruit on one condition: they must do it the troll way."

The trolls all opened their green mouths and laughed and laughed.

Nova and the other Sprouties looked at one another. What was going on?

"OK, little fairies," said Pa Troll. "We'll allow you to pick a tangfruit. Only one, mind you! And you must do it our way. None of this fairy flying business."

"No flying?" Lulu's eyes were wide. "We have to climb up there?"

The trolls grinned, showing their very green teeth. "No, you must use the Troll Slinger."

The trolls parted to reveal a strange contraption.

Two wooden poles jutted out from a platform, with a stretchy band strung between them.

"How does it work?" Coco asked. She sounded unusually nervous.

"We'll show you!" Rox jumped up on to the platform and leaned back into the stretchy band. Lex and Tex pulled the band back further and further ... then let go!

Rox was flung high into the air. She soared upwards, spinning a couple of times. Then, as she neared the top of the trees, she reached out and expertly grabbed a tangfruit. Moments later, she landed neatly on her wide green feet.

The trolls cheered.

"That's how it's done!" Pa Troll said, clapping Rox on the back. "Are you fairies too delicate to try it? You might get mud on your wings."

"We don't mind a bit of mud!" Nova assured the trolls. She turned to Lulu. "You should do this. You're the most acrobatic."

Lulu grimaced. "I can't tell the difference between ripe and unripe tangfruits – and neither can Zali or Coco. This one's up to you, Nova!"

9

Nova took a deep breath and approached the Troll Slinger. "After this, you might have to rename this thing the Fairy Flinger," she commented.

The trolls roared with laughter.

"You're pretty funny, little fairy." Rox looked impressed.

"You are," agreed Tex. "But let's see how good

you are with troll technology. Remember, no using those wings!"

Nova nodded as she stepped on to the platform. She tucked in her wings and leaned back into the stretchy band. Her pulse raced.

Can I do this?

But it was far too late to worry. Rox and Tex grabbed hold of the band and pulled it back. Nova felt the material stretch out behind her.

"Three, two, one, FAIRY FLING!" chanted the trolls.

Nova hurtled into the air. Over and over she cartwheeled, recovering just in time to see she was heading straight for the tangfruit tree!

Her eyes swept the branches. Was there a ripe one nearby? Yes! Quickly, she reached out and grabbed a juicy-looking star-shaped fruit.

"Got one!" she yelled, holding it up.

A shout of delight echoed around the valley. It wasn't just Nova's friends either – the trolls were also whooping!

But as Nova began to tumble towards the ground, the fruit slipped from her fingers.

"Lulu, catch!" Nova yelled.

In a heartbeat, Lulu sprang into the air and caught the precious fruit in one hand. She landed neatly just before Nova did – not quite so neatly. Nova skidded, tripped, somersaulted three times and ended up in a muddy patch.

"Are you OK?" Coco and Zali dashed over to help her up.

"I'm fine." Nova giggled, brushing off some mud. "That was so fun!"

Pa Troll was grinning. "You certainly proved that

fairies don't mind a bit of dirt on their wings!"

The trolls roared their funny, gravelly laughs.

Lex clapped Nova on the back. "Except for your landing, you did that as well as any troll. Didn't she, Pa?"

"She did," Pa Troll said. "And she's chosen a beauty of a tangfruit. That will soothe a lot of sore throats. It will cheer up those snufflebugs, too."

Nova tilted her head. "Tangfruit juice cheers you up?"

"If you mix it with dancing daisy pollen, it does. That's an old troll remedy."

"Are dancing daisies hard to find?" asked Nova.

"They're everywhere," said Lex. "There's a couple

of them right there." She pointed a green thumb.

Nova looked at her friends excitedly. "Imagine if we could cheer up those miserable snufflebugs as well as soothe their sore throats! Let's take some pollen back with us!" She looked back at the trolls. "If that's OK?"

"Go for it." Pa Troll chuckled. "If you can get it out, that is."

The Sprouties flew over to the daisies. The petals were tightly closed.

"Shall we try to prise one open?" Lulu suggested.

"Maybe we could shake the stems?" Coco said.

"No!" called Lex, hurrying over. "Dancing daisies only open when they hear birdsong. And not just any birdsong – it must be the call of the gleebird."

"The gleebird? Nova, that was the bird you imitated for us yesterday!" said Coco.

Zali grabbed hold of Nova's arm. "Can you remember it?"

"I think so." Nova closed her eyes. She knew they didn't have much time, but she wanted to get this right. Slowly, she began to whistle the gleebird's catchy tune.

Coco gasped. "The daisies are dancing!"

Still whistling, Nova opened her eyes. The long flower stems were swaying back and forth, exactly as if they were dancing! Even better – their petals were unfurling. Fat flecks of pollen drifted down as the daisies danced. It was raining pollen!

"Quick! Catch some!" yelped Coco.

Zali whipped off her hat and ran about, gathering pollen. "Vida said our hats would come in handy!"

Many of the trolls caught the pollen, too, using their big green hands to shovel the powder into their pockets.

"Is this enough?" Zali showed Nova her half-full hat.

Nova peered into the hat and stopped whistling. "More than enough," she declared. Taking a collecting tube from the bag, she carefully tipped in the pollen. But as she returned it to the bag, the tube of gold glitter fell out. It lay on the grass, shimmering in the sun.

A gasp rippled around the crowd of trolls.

"Glitter!" Pa Troll's eyes were shining almost as brightly as the glitter itself. "Where did you get it?"

"We grow it in our greenhouse." Nova was surprised at how excited the trolls were. Glitter was pretty, sure. But it was so common in the Forever Tree!

A thought struck her. "Would you like some? We have more than we need."

The trolls most definitely DID want glitter and quickly produced a little box. Nova gave the glitter tube a generous shake. The trolls gathered around the box, exclaiming with delight. "So much precious, precious glitter!"

"That's all the ingredients we need, right?" said

Coco. "Shall we get back?"

"Not a moment too soon!" Lulu zoomed into the air. "Goodbye, trolls. Thanks for the tangfruit."

"Come back anytime," called Pa Troll, who looked perfectly cheerful now. "Especially if you bring glitter."

Tex and Rox jumped up and down, waving happily, as the fairies fluttered away. "We'll be at the hospital burrow tomorrow morning," they called. "We've been working on a new act! It'll bring the house down."

The fairies waved back and zipped home to the Forever Tree. The good thing about the tree being so tall was that it was visible from almost anywhere in the forest!

Nova flapped her wings with all her might. She was determined to fly faster than she ever had.

"Nova, your extra fairy power has kicked in!" Zali cried as Nova overtook her. Even Coco couldn't keep up!

A few moments later, they arrived back at the tree. Lulu was first, but Nova's curly boots touched the ground not long after.

The waiting fairies erupted into loud cheers and whistles of delight. "The Sprouties are back!"

Quickly, the Sprout Wings fluttered over to the table that had been set up for them. It was covered with bowls and bottles and everything they might need. Nova laid out the ingredients they had collected.

Vida flew over. "I knew you'd find everything," she said, eyeing the huge tangfruit. "You're such clever Sprouties! And look who's come to watch."

On a low branch sat a number of patients from the hospital burrow, snuggled in blankets and surrounded by cushions. The little bunny was there, cuddling the carrot toy Zali had made her. The butterfly and the mouse and a few unwell fairies were there, too.

While Vida went back to the patients, the Sprout Wings got busy. They grated the fireroot and chopped and squeezed the tangfruit. Nova crushed up the leaf and measured the golden glitter.

"Who should do the move-and-mix spell?" asked Coco, once everything was ready.

"Nova," said Zali. "She's the best at it."

"Actually, I think we should do it together," Nova said. "We're forever friends, remember?"

Their friendship was starting to feel very powerful. Maybe it would help make their remedy even stronger!

The Sprout Wings pulled out their wands and held them above the bowl.

This will work, Nova thought. *I just know it will.* For the first time since she'd sprouted, Nova felt confident in her skills.

The friends each touched the ingredients with

their wands and made the magical shapes in the air. With a twinkle of light, all the ingredients disappeared. A moment later, they appeared in the bowl.

"Halfway there!" Zali said. "Now for the mix. Hope I don't mess it up."

"We'll be fine." Nova smiled at her friends. "Everyone ready? I'll count us in."

On the count of three, the fairies tapped the side of the bowl and made the stirring motion with their wands. Instantly, the ingredients crumbled and began to mix. The glitter gave the remedy a rich, golden gleam.

The fairies leaned forward and breathed in deeply.

"It smells wonderful," said Coco.

"Like magic," said Zali.

"And friendship," added Nova. "If that has a smell." She pulled out the tube of daisy pollen and took a sniff. Just smelling the pollen made Nova feel more cheerful. "Shall we add the final, extra special ingredient?"

Her friends nodded, so Nova took a big pinch of dancing daisy pollen and sprinkled it into the mixture. It quickly dissolved.

There was no going back now! Would this half-fairy, half-troll remedy actually work?

"It's officially time to assess today's remedy!" Vida announced. "Sprout Wings, please take your potion over to the judges."

Nova, Coco, Lulu and Zali flew over to the floating platform. Nova held out the bowl with shaking hands. Nervously, she placed it on the table. "Here is our sore throat remedy."

With a flourish, the Shimmerbud elder removed

a single white flower from her hair and dipped it into the potion. "If the flower turns pink," she explained, "it means your remedy is successful."

A hush fell over the crowd. It felt as though every single fairy was holding their breath!

Finally, the elder pulled the flower out and held it aloft. Nova thought her heart might explode. The flower had not turned pink. It was a deep shade of purple.

"Ooooooh!" The watching fairies twittered and whispered among themselves.

The elders exchanged a look.

"Oh my!" the Flutterfly elder murmured. "It's been a long time since we've had a purple reaction."

"But what does that mean?" asked Coco, a note of uncertainty in her usually confident voice.

Instead of answering, the Shimmerbud elder asked a question of her own. "Did you follow the recipe exactly?"

"No," admitted Nova. Her face felt hot. Had they made a terrible mistake? "I added dancing daisy pollen."

The elder nodded thoughtfully. "How interesting. I never would have thought of using dancing daisy."

"We heard that it cheers up patients while also fixing their sore throats," Nova explained. "We, um, thought the snufflebugs could do with some cheering up."

"Don't look worried," said the Twinklestar elder kindly. "A purple reaction is not a bad thing. It means you have created a powerful new remedy."

"One that hasn't been made by fairykind before," added the Sparkleberry elder.

"It's a huge achievement, particularly for Sprout Wings," concluded the Shimmerbud elder. "Remarkable, really."

A Shimmerbud fairy approached with the basket of sneezing snufflebugs. "Who would like to give the snufflebugs their remedy? Three drops each."

"Can I?" Coco asked.

The others nodded and Coco carefully gave the bugs a dose. The reaction was immediate!

The red faded from their tiny noses, their coughing stopped and, after a moment, so did the sneezing. And the biggest change of all? They were smiling!

"I feel amazing!" cried one.

"I feel amazinger," declared the other.

The little bugs flung off the scarves that Zali had made and did the happy dance of the no-longer sick. Their multiple legs went in all directions.

"They're *shuffle*bugs now!" joked Nova. She felt like doing a happy dance herself.

Everyone laughed.

"I've never seen such gleeful bugs in all my time," the Shimmerbud elder said. "Adding dancing daisy pollen was an excellent decision."

"It was Nova's idea," said Coco.

Nova shook her head. "It's all thanks to the trolls. They make their cold remedy from wild tangfruit and dancing daisies."

"You should see the size of their tangfruit! They're this big!" Zali stretched her arms wide.

"Maybe not quite that big," Nova said, laughing, "but they're much, much bigger and healthier than in our greenhouse."

Once again, the elders exchanged a look.

"There was a time when fairies and trolls did a lot of trade," the Flutterfly elder said. "Perhaps it's time we restart that tradition."

"I wonder if we grow anything that the trolls would like?" mused the Sparkleberry elder.

The Sprout Wings grinned at one another. They knew the answer to that!

"Glitter!" they chorused.

"Of course! And no one grows glitterplants like we do," said the Twinklestar elder. "Tangfruits for glitter – an excellent exchange!"

"You did well to listen and learn from the trolls," the Shimmerbud elder said. "But the potion you have made is *not* the Forever Fairy Sore Throat Remedy."

Nova froze. Were they about to fail the trial, despite their remedy working?

The elder went on. "This potion is something better. As such, I think it deserves a new name. I propose we call it the Forever Fairy and Troll Sore Throat Remedy. And congratulations – I am happy to announce you have all passed the Shimmerbud trial."

The Sprouties beamed at one another. Their remedy had worked, and they'd completed their second trial. Nova felt like she was shimmering with pride!

The Twinklestar elder cleared her throat. "You may hold up your wands."

Nova and the others did, and a new image appeared just below the wings symbol on their wands: a tiny flower.

The Twinklestar elder smoothed down her silver-and-gold robes. "You have certainly earned the rest of the day off, Sprout Wings. But don't forget – you have two trials remaining. The next one is for my pod."

"We can't wait!" Coco yelled, pulling the others into a hug.

Nova felt a warmth spreading through her. She was so lucky to have Coco, Lulu and Zali as her sprout mates!

ABOUT THE AUTHORS

Maddy Mara is the pen name of Australian creative duo Hilary Rogers and Meredith Badger. Hilary and Meredith have been making children's books together for many years, including the *Forever Fairies*, *Dragon Games*, and *Dragon Girls* series. They love dreaming up new ideas and always have lots of projects bubbling away. When not writing, Hilary can be found cooking weird things or going on long walks, often with Meredith. And Meredith can be found teaching English online all around the world or daydreaming about being able to fly. They both currently live in Melbourne, Australia.

Find out more at maddymara.com.

Turn the page for a special sneak

peek of Coco's fairy adventure!

"This is the test kitchen," the troll explained. "Fairies try all kinds of new recipes in here. I wouldn't taste that without knowing what it is. Anything could happen."

Coco grinned. "Really? *Anything?*"

He nodded. "Not so long ago, I became the first-ever blue troll after doing what you were about to do."

Coco clapped her hand over her mouth. "Oh no!"

"Oh yes," said the troll. "The Twinklestars were experimenting with too-blue-berries. I took one sip of the syrup, and I still have a blue tongue."

He stuck out his tongue. It really was blue.

Coco tried hard not to giggle – but it was impossible. "Your poor thing!"

The troll shrugged. "It was tasty. I'm Pix, by the way."

"I'm Coco," said Coco, shaking hands. Her hand was half the size of the troll's. "I have a lot of questions. Like, how did you get in here? And, even more importantly, *why* are you in here?"

Pix patted a curl of rope attached to his belt. "If we have rope, trolls can get just about anywhere," he said proudly. "As for your second question, I'm here for the same reason you are: tasty things to eat. How about we whip up a snack?"

Forever Fairies

Forever fairies ... and forever friends!

DRAGON GIRLS

THE GLITTER DRAGONS

DRAGON GIRLS

**Azmina the Gold
Glitter Dragon**

Maddy Mara

THE GLITTER DRAGONS

DRAGON GIRLS

**Willa the Silver
Glitter Dragon**

Maddy Mara

THE GLITTER DRAGONS

DRAGON GIRLS

**Naomi the Rainbow
Glitter Dragon**

Maddy Mara

THE TREASURE DRAGONS

DRAGON GIRLS

**Mei the Ruby
Treasure Dragon**

Maddy Mara

THE TREASURE DRAGONS

DRAGON GIRLS

**Aisha the Sapphire
Treasure Dragon**

Maddy Mara

THE TREASURE DRAGONS

DRAGON GIRLS

**Quinn the Jade
Treasure Dragon**

Maddy Mara

Collect them all!

DRAGON GAMES

PLAY THE GAME. SAVE THE REALM.